NFL TEAM STORIES

The Story of the

WASHINGTON REDSKINS

By Jim Gigliotti

Kaleidoscope
Minneapolis, MN

The Quest for Discovery Never Ends

•••

This edition first published in 2021 by Kaleidoscope Publishing, Inc.

No part of this publication may be reproduced in whole or in part without written permission of the publisher.

For information regarding permission, write to Kaleidoscope Publishing, Inc. 6012 Blue Circle Drive Minnetonka, MN 55343

Library of Congress Control Number 2020936061

ISBN 978-1-64519-249-7 (library bound) 978-1-64519-317-3 (ebook)

Text copyright © 2021 by Kaleidoscope Publishing, Inc. All-Star Sports, Bigfoot Books, and associated logos are trademarks and/or registered trademarks of Kaleidoscope Publishing, Inc.

Printed in the United States of America.

Bigfoot lurks within one of the images in this book. It's up to you to find him!

TABLE OF CONTENTS

Kickoff! 4

Chapter 1: Redskins History 6

Chapter 2: Redskins All-Time Greats 16

Chapter 3: Redskins Superstars 22

    Beyond the Book 28

    Research Ninja 29

    Further Resources 30

    Glossary 31

    Index 32

    Photo Credits 32

    About the Author 32

KICKOFF!

"Hail to the Redskins! Hail vic-tor-eeee!"

The crowd at Washington's home field is on its feet. The fans are singing! The Redskins were the first NFL team with a **fight song**. Washington fans still sing it every time the team scores. That did not happen too often in 2019. The Redskins scored fewer points than any other team in the league. But the team has a new coach. It has some good young players. The fans hope to sing again soon!

Washington fans dress as "Hogs." The cheese is for a visiting Packers fan!

Chapter 1
Redskins History

The Redskins began play in 1932. They were in Boston and were called the Braves. The city had a baseball team also called the Braves. Several NFL teams were named after baseball teams. The NFL's Braves became the Redskins in 1933. The team moved to Washington D.C. in 1937. The team's first owner was George Preston Marshall. He was an important owner in the early years of the NFL. He is in the Hall of Fame.

FUN FACT
Washington owner George Marshall made a lot of money in the laundry business!

Star QB Sammy Baugh (center) celebrates with teammates.

Sammy Baugh

Washington fans didn't wait long for a title. The Redskins won the NFL championship their first year in D.C.! Sammy Baugh was the star. He was a big-time quarterback. He was great on defense, too. Many players played both offense and defense in those days. Baugh was even the NFL's best punter! The Redskins won another title in 1942. Baugh was the hero again that year.

TWO-SPORT STAR

"Slingin' Sammy" Baugh was a great baseball player, too. He played in baseball's minor leagues after the 1937 football season ended. That is how he got his famous nickname. It was for the way he threw a baseball.

Joe Theismann in Super Bowl XVII

Baugh **retired** after 1952. It was a long time before the Redskins were great again. They did not make the playoffs in the 1950s or 1960s. They had a good run in the 1970s, though. They made the playoffs five times from 1971-76. Those Redskins used many older players. They were called the "Over-the-Hill Gang." That's a nickname for people who might be too old for their job. The Over-the-Hill Gang made it to the Super Bowl in 1972!

The Redskins won their first Super Bowl in 1982. They were champs again in '87. They won it all in '91, too. That made it three Super Bowls in 10 seasons! They were the first team to win three with different quarterbacks.

Joe Theismann was a big, tough passer. He threw two TD passes to help Washington win Super Bowl XVII. Doug Williams led the Redskins to the top five years later. (See pages 14-15.) In 1992, Mark Rypien became the third Washington Super Bowl QB.

Washington used different QBs. But all three champions had the same head coach: Joe Gibbs.

Joe Gibbs and his three Super Bowl trophies

Gibbs retired after 1992. He returned to the team in 2004. He led the Redskins to the playoffs twice more. He retired for good after 2007. Things have been tough for the team since then. A rare highlight came in 2015. Washington won the NFC East Division for only the second time in the 2000s.

The Redskins hit bottom in 2019. They lost nine of their first 10 games. In the final game of the season, they were whomped by the Dallas Cowboys 47–10.

Washington **hired** Ron Rivera as coach for 2020. Rivera was coach of the Carolina Panthers for nine seasons. He led that team to the playoffs four times. Can he do that in Washington, too?

Dallas and Washington are NFC East rivals.

TIMELINE OF THE WASHINGTON REDSKINS

1932

1932: The team begins play as the Boston Braves.

1937

1937: The Redskins move to Washington D.C. and win the NFL title.

1942

1942: Washington wins its second league title.

1982

1982: The Redskins win the Super Bowl for the first time.

1991

1991: The team wins its third Super Bowl in 10 seasons.

2012

2012: The Redskins win the NFC East for the first time in 13 years.

WHAT A QUARTER

In 1987, Washington was doing pretty well. Jay Schroeder was the QB. Still, the coaches thought the Redskins could do better. They promoted Doug Williams to be the starter. It proved to be a great move.

Washington beat Chicago in the first round of the playoffs. Williams had a TD pass. He had two more to beat the Vikings. That sent Washington to Super Bowl XXII. The Denver Broncos took a 10–0 lead. Then Williams really went to work.

In the second quarter, he threw an incredible four touchdown passes! He hit Ricky Sanders on an 80-yard bomb. Gary Clark caught a short TD pass. After Timmy Smith ran for a 58-yard score, Williams connected with Sanders again. Williams hit Clint Didier for the fifth TD of the quarter.

It was one of the best performances ever in the NFL's biggest game. Williams was a star. He was also a pioneer. He was the first African American to start a Super Bowl at quarterback. Many more have come after him, inspired by his success. The backup had become the hero!

Chapter 2
Redskins All-Time Greats

Sammy Baugh was the biggest star in Washington's early days. Other great quarterbacks followed him. Norm Snead and Sonny Jurgensen made the **Pro Bowl** six times in the 1960s. Billy Kilmer was a Pro Bowl QB in the 1970s. Joe Theismann was an all-star in the 1980s.

Theismann's top receiver was Art Monk. He caught 106 passes in 1984. That was an NFL record. Monk was the league's all-time leading receiver when he **retired** after 1995. He is still the Redskins' top pass catcher.

FUN FACT
Art Monk's 12,026 receiving yards are still a Redskins record.

"Run, Riggo, run!" That was the cry for the Redskins in the 1980s. "Riggo" was John Riggins. The big fullback also was called "Diesel." He was as powerful as a truck. Riggins is the team's all-time leading rusher. He was at his best in the 1982 playoffs. He gained more than 100 yards four games in a row.

In Super Bowl XVII that season, Riggins made a famous run. Washington faced a fourth down. They needed one yard to make a first down. They gave the ball to Riggins. He found a hole in the line and looked upfield. Miami defensive back Don McNeal zoomed in to make the tackle. Riggins bashed over him! Then "Riggo" turned on the speed. He rumbled 43 yards for a huge touchdown!

Riggins ran behind a powerful line nicknamed the "Hogs." The Hogs led the way for several more 1,000-yard rushers. Russ Grimm, Joe Jacoby, and Mark May were important Hogs.

Joe Jacoby

FUN FACT

Riggins led the NFL in 1983 with an incredible 24 rushing TDs.

The Redskins have had some great players on defense, too. Cornerback Darrell Green might have been the best. One reason was his great speed. Green could catch up with the fastest receivers. His great play helped him make the Pro Bowl seven times. Today, he is in the Hall of Fame.

Green **intercepted** 54 passes in his career. That is the most in team history. Chris Hanburger made the most tackles. He was a star on the playoff teams of the 1970s. Dexter Manley had the most **sacks**. He played on two teams that won the Super Bowl.

Darrell Green

REDSKINS
RECORDS

These players piled up the best stats in Redskins history. The numbers are career records through the 2019 season.

Total TDs: Charley Taylor, 90

TD Passes: Sammy Baugh, 187

Passing Yards: Joe Theismann, 25,206

Rushing Yards: John Riggins, 7,472

Receptions: Art Monk, 888

Points: Mark Moseley, 1,206

Sacks: Dexter Manley, 91

Chapter 3
Redskins Superstars

Today's Redskins have high hopes for their young players. One is QB Dwayne Haskins. Washington **drafted** him in the first round in 2019. Haskins helped make Ohio State one of college football's top teams.

Terry McLaurin was only a third-round draft pick. Yet as a rookie, he was Washington's leader in catches and receiving yards.

The young passer took over as the starter late in 2019. He showed fans some great moves. They hope to sing more about him in the future!

In college, Haskins threw passes to receiver Terry McLaurin. The two teamed up in the NFL, too. The Redskins drafted McLaurin in 2019, too. McLaurin became Haskins' top target in Washington. The Redskins hope they are teammates for a long time.

Dwayne Haskins

Brandon Scherff could be as good as the famous Hogs. The Redskins drafted him in the first round in 2015. He became a starting guard right away. Scherff made the Pro Bowl for the third time in '19. He helped **veteran** runner Adrian Peterson gain more than 1,000 yards rushing and receiving. Scherff has a couple of young backs to block for in 2020. Derrius Guice and Bryce Love are just getting started. The Redskins hope they give the offense a boost.

Brandon Scherff

Adrian Peterson

Landon Collins

Safety Landon Collins is a star on defense. He has strength. That lets him tackle ball carriers near the **line of scrimmage**. He has speed. That lets him cover receivers in the open field. Collins was an all-star three times with the rival Giants. He signed with the Redskins in 2019.

Linebacker Montez Sweat is a key player. The Redskins drafted him in the first round in '19. Sweat had seven sacks as a rookie. Veteran Ryan Kerrigan has four seasons with 10 or more sacks. He hopes to get another in 2020.

On offense and defense, Washington hopes it gives fans something to sing about!

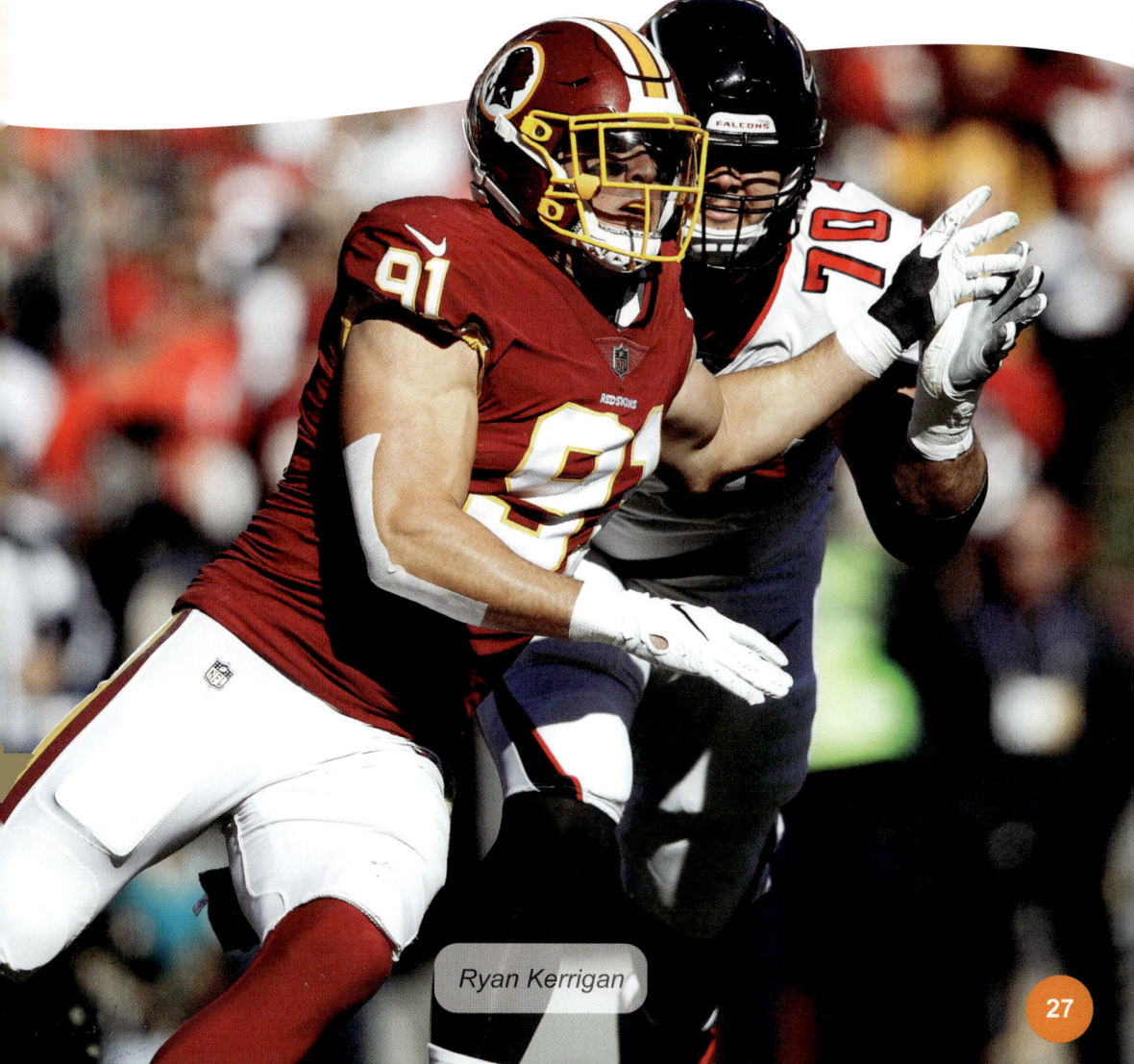

Ryan Kerrigan

BEYOND THE BOOK

After reading the book, it's time to think about what you learned. Try the following exercises to jumpstart your ideas.

RESEARCH

FIND OUT MORE. Where would you go to find out more about your favorite NFL teams and players? Check out NFL.com, of course. Each team also has its own website. What other sports information sites can you find? See if you can find other cool facts about your favorite team.

CREATE

GET ARTISTIC. Each NFL team has a logo. The Redskins logo shows a Native American spear. Get some art materials and try designing your own logo for the team. Or create a new team and make a logo for it. What colors would you choose? How would you draw the mascot?

DISCOVER

GO DEEP! This book is about a team with a name that many people think is wrong. Read more about the issue of the Washington NFL team's name and why people are upset. What does the team say? What do people against the name say? What do you think should be done?

GROW

GET OUT AND PLAY! You don't need to be in the NFL to enjoy football. You just need a football and some friends. Play touch or tag football. Or you can hang cloth flags from your belt; grab the belt and make the "tackle." See who has the best arm to be quarterback. Who is the best receiver? Who can run the fastest? Time to play football!

RESEARCH NINJA

Visit *www.ninjaresearcher.com/2497* to learn how to take your research skills and book report writing to the next level!

RESEARCH

DIGITAL LITERACY TOOLS

SEARCH LIKE A PRO
Learn about how to use search engines to find useful websites.

FACT OR FAKE?
Discover how you can tell a trusted website from an untrustworthy resource.

TEXT DETECTIVE
Explore how to zero in on the information you need most.

SHOW YOUR WORK
Research responsibly—learn how to cite sources.

WRITE

GET TO THE POINT
Learn how to express your main ideas.

PLAN OF ATTACK
Learn prewriting exercises and create an outline.

DOWNLOADABLE REPORT FORMS

Further Resources

BOOKS

Editors of Sports Illustrated Kids. *1st and 10 (Revised and Updated): Top 10 Lists of Everything in Football*. New York: Sports Illustrated Kids, 2016.

Storm, Marysa. *Highlights of the Washington Redskins*. Mankato, Minn.: Black Rabbit Books, 2019.

Whiting, Jim. *The Story of the Washington Redskins (NFL Today)*. Mankato, Minn.: Creative Paperbacks, 2019.

WEBSITES

Factsurfer.com gives you a safe, fun way to find more information.

1. Go to www.factsurfer.com.
2. Enter "Washington Redskins" into the search box and click 🔍
3. Select your book cover to see a list of related websites.

Glossary

drafted: chosen in the NFL's annual selection of college players for NFL teams. Dwayne Haskins was the first player Washington drafted in 2019.

fight song: a tune sung by fans of a team. "Hail to the Redskins!" is one of the NFL's oldest fight songs.

hired: given a job by a company or a team. When Washington hired Joe Gibbs, they made the right choice!

intercepted: caught by the defense. Quentin Dunbar intercepted the pass thrown by Tom Brady.

line of scrimmage: the point where each play starts. Controlling the line of scrimmage is a good way for offenses to pile up yards.

Pro Bowl: The NFL's annual all-star game. Washington punter Tress Way made the NFC Pro Bowl team for 2019.

retired: left a job or team after a long period of service. When Joe Gibbs retired, Washington had big shoes to fill!

sack: tackle made of the QB behind the line of scrimmage. Matthew Ioannidis led Washington with 8.5 sacks in 2019.

veteran: a player with many years of service. With 12 years in the NFL, Adrian Peterson is one of the team's oldest veterans.

Index

Baugh, "Slingin'" Sammy, 9, 10, 16
Boston Braves, 6
Carolina Panthers, 12
Clark, Gary, 15
Collins, Landon, 26
Dallas Cowboys, 12
Didier, Clint, 15
Gibbs, Joe, 11, 12
Green, Darrell, 20
Grimm, Russ, 18
Guice, Derrius, 24
Hanburger, Chris, 20
Haskins, Dwayne, 22, 23
"Hogs, The," 5, 18, 24
Jacoby, Joe, 18
Kerrigan, Ryan, 27
Kilmer, Billy, 16
Love, Bryce, 24
Manley, Dexter, 20
Marshall, George Preston, 6
May, Mark, 18
McLaurin, Terry, 23
McNeal, Don, 18
Monk, Art, 16
"Over-the-Hill Gang," 10
Peterson, Adrian, 24
Riggins, John, 18
Rivera, Ron, 12
Rypien, Mark, 11
Sanders, Ricky, 15
Scherff, Brandon, 24
Smith, Timmy, 15
Snead, Norm, 16
Super Bowl, 10, 11, 15, 18, 20
Sweat, Montez, 27
Theismann, Joe, 11, 16
Williams, Doug, 11, 15

PHOTO CREDITS

The images in this book are reproduced through the courtesy of: AP Images: Paul Spinelli 4, 19; 6; 8; Pro Football Hall of Fame 9; Tony Tomsic 10; Elise Amendola 14; David Longstreath 16; Al Messerschmidt 18. Focus on Football: 25, 27. Newscom: Roger Wollenberg 11; Michael Smith/UPI 20; Tim Tai/TNS 23; Kyle Ross/Icon SW 22; Frank Jansky/Icon SW 24; Mark Goldman/Icon SW 26. **Cover photo:** Focus on Football.

About the Author

Jim Gigliotti was an editor at NFL Publishing for many years. Now he writes books for young readers.